me

Treasure Chest Readers

Mars Mouse

Text by Janine Scott
Illustrations by Hannah Wood

Published in 2010 by Windmill Books, LLC
303 Park Avenue South, Suite # 1280, New York, NY 10010-3657

Adaptations to North American Edition © 2010 Windmill Books, Copyright © 2008 by Autumn Publishing

Published in 2008 by Autumn Publishing, A division of Bonnier Media Ltd., Chichester, West Sussex, PO20 7EQ, UK

CREDITS: Text by Janine Scott, Illustrations by Deborah Rigby

Library of Congress Cataloging-in-Publication Data

Scott, Janine.
 Mars mouse / text by Janine Scott ; illustrations by Hannah Wood. -- 1st North American ed.
    p. cm. -- (Treasure chest readers)
 Published in Great Britain in 2008 by Autumn Publishing.
 Summary: Equipped with a backpack rocket, hungry Mars Mouse searches for cheese in deep space and finally lands on the Moon much to the distress of the Man in the Moon.
 ISBN 978-1-60754-676-4 (library binding) -- ISBN 978-1-60754-677-1 (pbk.) -- ISBN 978-1-60754-678-8 (6-pack)
 [1. Stories in rhyme. 2. Outer space--Fiction. 3. Mice--Fiction. 4. Cheese--Fiction. 5. Moon--Fiction. 6. Humorous stories.] I. Wood, Hannah, ill. II. Title.
 PZ8.3.S4275Mar 2010
 [E]--dc22
                              2009040142

Manufactured in the United States of America

CPSIA Compliance Information: Batch #BW01W: For further information contact Windmill Books, New York, New York at 1-866-478-0556.

alphabet
s o u p ™
an imprint of
WINDMILL BOOKS ™
New York

Just the size of a pocket
With a backpack rocket,
Mars Mouse hunts for cheese in deep space.

He zooms past stars
To cafés near and far,
And no one can keep up with his pace.

The Man in the Moon
Had been watching since June
And guarding his home every night.

Its cheesy bright glow,
A yummy yellow,
Was ripe for Mars Mouse's bite.

And hungry Mars Mouse
Did get to Moon House
And started to nibble and gnaw.

He ate the cheese stairs,
He ate the cheese chairs,
Then started to chew the front door.

The mouse nibbled and crunched
Till the ceiling was munched
And the walls were Swiss-cheesy with holes.

"This moon is so pleasant.
I'll make it a crescent,"
Said the mouse as he gnawed to his goal.

The Man in the Moon
Then started to swoon.
He knew that the mouse must be banished.

That hungry Mars Mouse
Had eaten his house,
And much of the moon had just vanished.

The Man in the Moon
Felt he had to act soon.
His moon was now only a sliver.

He left his cheese house
In search of the mouse.
With a firm word to deliver!

He soon found the robber
By following the slobber
And the smell of the stinkiest cheese.

For Mars Mouse now dribbled
As he gnawed and he nibbled,
And slept off his munching at ease.

When Mars tried to fly
Way up in the sky,
He found he was frightfully fat.

He was simple to snatch,
A real easy catch.
But that wasn't the end of that.

The Man in the Moon
Gave Mars Mouse a spoon
And ordered some cheese to take out.

He made that Mars Mouse
Fix up his Moon House
By spreading the cheese all about.

Mars Mouse had soon
Made him a new moon,
Which takes us right up to the present.

Now Mars's monthly chore
Is to nibble and gnaw
The round moon right into a crescent.

But he never eats
Cheesy moon treats
When the moon should be full and round.

He has learned to say,
"No cheese today!
That's more than enough I have found!"

Now his name is Moon Mouse
With his own cheesy house
And moon cheese for lunch and for dinner.

And each month he fasts
While the full moon lasts,
Then it's time for the moon to get thinner!

LEARN MORE! READ MORE!

The *Mars Mouse* story features lots of rhythm and rhyme. Rhythm and rhyme can help you expand your reading universe. Here are some more books that use and explore some of those great reading tools.

FICTION
Berkes, Marianne. *Over in the Jungle: A Rainforest Rhyme.* Nevada City, CA: Dawn Publications, 2007.

Dewdney, Anna. *Llama Llama Red Pajama.* New York: Viking Juvenile, 2005.

NONFICTION
Prelutsky, Jack. *Read a Rhyme, Write a Rhyme.* New York: Dragonfly Books, 2009.

For more great fiction and nonfiction, go to
www.windmillbooks.com.

WITHDRAWN